D0522076

For Vivienne
who laid this path

First published 1992
by Walker Books Ltd, 87 Vauxhall Walk
London SE11 5HJ

© 1992 Camilla Ashforth

First printed 1992
Printed and bound in Hong Kong by
South China Printing Co. (1988) Ltd

British Library Cataloguing in Publication Data
A catalogue record for this book is available
from the British Library.

ISBN 0-7445-2114-9

HORATIO'S BED

Camilla Ashforth

WALKER BOOKS
LONDON

All night Horatio could not sleep.

He tossed and turned,

and wriggled,

and rolled.

But he just could not get comfortable.
I'll go and ask James what's the matter,
he thought.

James was busy drawing.
Horatio sat down. "I couldn't sleep
all night," he said.
"Is it your bed?" asked James.
"I haven't got a bed," Horatio said.
"Then let's make you one," said James.

James took a clean sheet of paper
from his Useful Box and very
carefully drew a bed for Horatio.
It was a big square bed with a leg
at each corner.
Then he took another sheet of paper
and drew another bed for Horatio.
This one was a big square bed with a
leg at each corner too.

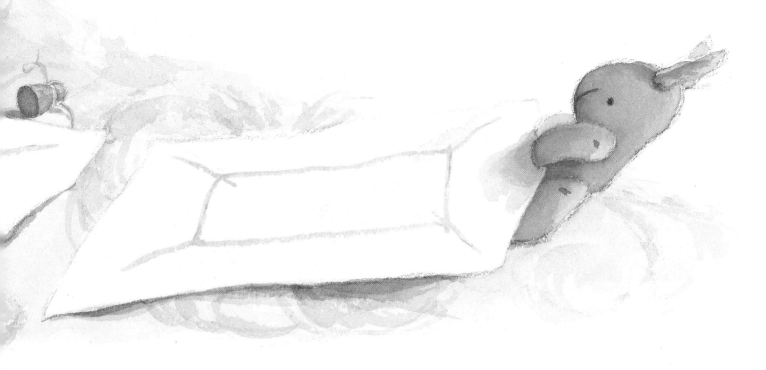

Horatio was very excited.
He took one of James's drawings
and tried to fold it into a bed.

Then he climbed inside it and
closed his eyes.

It wasn't very comfortable and
when Horatio rolled over …
R R R I I I P P P !

James looked up.
"That bed looks too hard to sleep on,"
he said and carried on with his drawing.

Horatio thought for a moment.
Then he pulled some feathers out of
James's pillow and made a big square
bed with them.

But when he lay on it the feathers
tickled his nose.

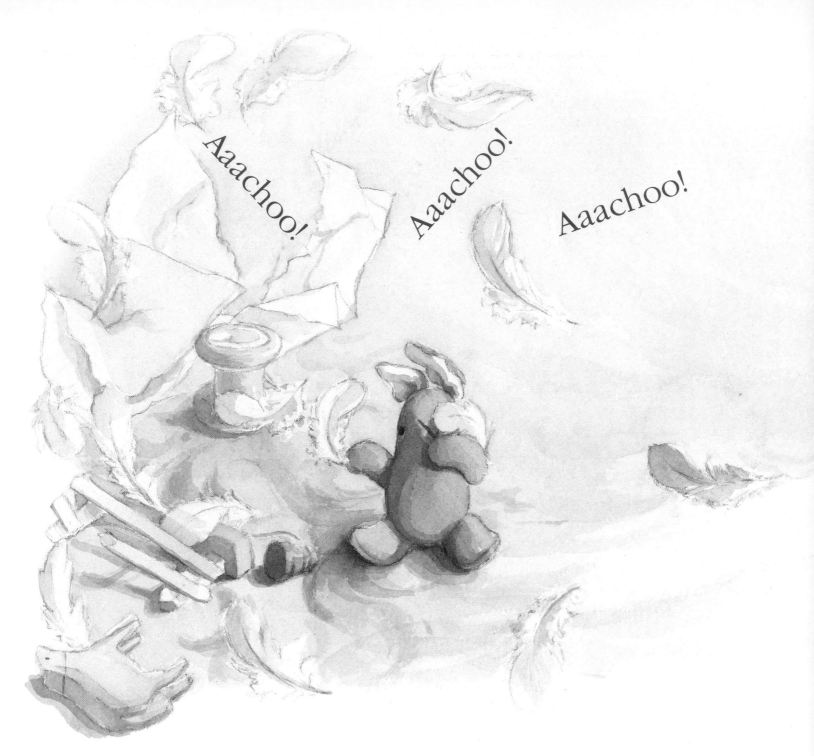

Aaachoo!

Aaachoo!

Aaachoo!

He sneezed and sneezed.

James put down his pencil and
blew away the feathers.

James sat Horatio down on
his Useful Box.
"You wait here a minute," he said,
"while I just finish drawing your bed."
He had already drawn five square beds
and was getting rather good at them.

But when James turned away,
Horatio slipped down from
the Useful Box. He wanted to
see what James kept inside.

He made some steps
up to the lid.

He pushed it open
and leaned in.
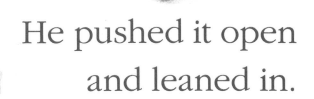

There were all sorts of things – buttons,
brushes, keys and clothes pegs, clock
wheels, clips and little bits of string.

Horatio looked for a bed.
He couldn't find anything that
looked like James's drawings.

But he did find a big red sock.
"Look, James!" he cried. "I've found
your other sock!"

James did not seem very pleased.
He didn't like anyone looking
in his Useful Box.
Not even Horatio.

Very quietly and carefully he started
to put away his Useful Bits.

When he had finished, he closed the
lid and looked for Horatio.
"Now we can make you
a bed," he said.

But there was no need,
because Horatio was fast asleep.
His bed was not square and it did
not have a leg at each corner.
But for little Horatio
it was just right.